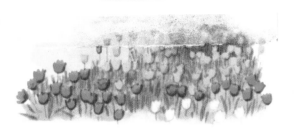

Hippocrene

CHILDREN'S
ILLUSTRATED
CROATIAN
DICTIONARY

ENGLISH - CROATIAN
CROATIAN - ENGLISH

Compiled by the Editors of Hippocrene Books

Croatian language translation by Liliana Pavicic

Interior Illustrations by S. Grant (24, 81, 88); J. Gress (page 10, 21, 24, 37, 46, 54, 59, 65, 72, 75, 77); K. Migliorelli (page 13, 14, 18, 19, 20, 22, 25, 31, 32, 37, 39, 40, 46, 47, 66, 71, 72, 73, 75, 77, 78, 79, 83); N. Zhukov (page 8, 13, 14, 17, 23, 27, 29, 33, 34, 39, 40, 41, 52, 64, 65, 71, 72, 73, 78, 84, 86, 88).
Cover image of Croatians © JUPITERIMAGES, and its licensors. All rights reserved.

Design, prepress, and production by Graafiset International, Inc.

Cataloging-in-Publication data available from the Library of Congress.

ISBN: 0-7818-1076-0

Printed in China

For information address:
Hippocrene Books, Inc.
171 Madison Avenue
New York, NY 10016
www.hippocrenebooks.com

INTRODUCTION

With their absorbent minds, infinite curiosities and excellent memories, children have enormous capacities to master many languages. All they need is exposure and encouragement.

The easiest way to learn a foreign language is to simulate the same natural method by which a child learns English. The natural technique is built on the concept that language is representational of concrete objects and ideas. The use of pictures and words are the natural way for children to begin to acquire a new language.

The concept of this Illustrated Dictionary is to allow children to build vocabulary and initial competency naturally. Looking at the pictorial content of the Dictionary and saying and matching the words in connection to the drawings gives children the opportunity to discover the foreign language and thus, a new way to communicate.

The drawings in the Dictionary are designed to capture children's imaginations and make the learning process interesting and entertaining, as children return to a word and picture repeatedly until they begin to recognize it.

The beautiful images and clear presentation make this dictionary a wonderful tool for unlocking your child's multilingual potential.

Deborah Dumont, M.A., M.Ed.,
Child Psychologist and Educational Consultant

PAGE 4 IS BLANK

Croatian Pronunciation

Letter(s)	Pronunciation system used
A (a)	**ah** like the a in English "art"
B (b)	**b** as in English "baby"
C (c)	**ts** as in English "nuts"
Č (č)	**chu** as in English "church"
Ć (ć)	**ch** as in English "cherry"
D (d)	**d** as in English "dog"
Đ (đ)	**j** as in English "jacket"
Dž (dž)	**dg** as in English "edge"
E (e)	**ay** as in English "air"
F (f)	**f** as in English "father"
G (g)	**g** as in English "good"
H (h)	**h** as in English "happy"
I (i)	**ee** as in English "green"
J (j)	**y** as in English "you"
K (k)	**k** as in English "kitten"
L (l)	**l** as in English "love"
Lj (lj)	**lya** as in English "million"
M (m)	**m** as in English "mother"
N (n)	**n** as in English "nose"
Nj (nj)	**nya** as in English "onion"
O (o)	**o** as in English "boat"
P (p)	**p** as in English "park"
R (r)	**rr** as in English "marry"
S (s)	**s** as in English "sun"
Š (š)	**sh** as in English "shell"
T (t)	**t** as in English "table"
U (u)	**oo** as in English "shoe"
V (v)	**v** as in English "vase"
Z (z)	**z** as in English "zero"
Ž (ž)	**zh** as in English "television"

airplane   **zrakoplov**
zra-ko-plov

alligator   **aligator**
ah-li-ga-tor

alphabet   **abeceda**
ah-be-tse-dah

antelope   **antilopa**
ahn-tee-lohpa

antlers   **rogovi**
roh-go-vee

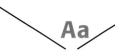

apple　　　　　　**jabuka**
ya-boo-kah

aquarium　　　　　**akvarij**
ah-kvar-eeyi

arch　　　　　　　**luk**
l-ook

arrow　　　　　　**strijela**
st-ree-yela

autumn　　　　　　**jesen**
ye-sen

baby   **beba**
beh-ba

backpack   **ruksak**
rook-sak

badger   **jazavac**
ya-za-vats

baker   **pekar**
peh-kar

ball   **lopta**
lohp-tah

balloon   **balon**
bah-lohn

banana

banana
ba-na-na

barley

ječam
ye-chum

barrel

bačva
bah-chva

basket

košara
koh-shahrah

bat

šišmiš
sheesh-meesh

beach

plaža
plah-zhah

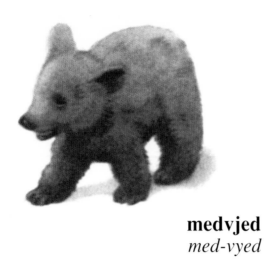

bear **medvjed**
med-vyed

beaver **dabar**
dah-bar

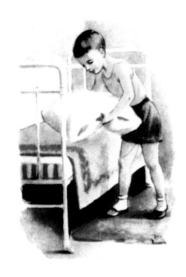

bed **krevet**
kreh-vet

bee **pčela**
pch-ella

beetle **buba**
boo-bah

bell **zvono**
zvoh-noh

belt   **pojas**
poh-yas

bench   **klupa**
kloo-pah

bicycle   **bicikl**
bee-tsee-kul

binoculars   **dalekozor**
dah-leko-zor

bird   **ptica**
ptee-sa

birdcage   **ptičji kavez**
pteech-i-yee kah-vez

black　　　　　　　　**crno**
tsrnoh

blocks　　　　　　　**kocke**
kots-keh

blossom　　　　　　**cvijet**
ts-vuh-yet

blue　　　　　　　　**plavo**
pla-voh

boat　　　　　　　　**lađa**
lah-dzah

bone　　　　　　　　**kost**
kohst

book   **knjiga**
                       kny-eegah

boot   **čizma**
                       cheez-mah

bottle   **boca**
                       bots-ah

bowl   **zdjela**
                       zdyella

boy   **dječak**
                       dye-chak

bracelet   **narukvica**
                       nah-rook-veetsa

branch   **grana**
grahna

bread   **kruh**
kroo-h

breakfast   **doručak**
dohr-u-chak

bridge   **most**
mohst

broom   **metla**
met-lah

brother   **brat**
brah-t

brown   **smeđe**
smedge-eh

brush   **četka**
chet-kah

bucket   **kanta**
kahn-tah

bulletin board   **oglasna ploča**
oh-gloss-nah ploh-cha

bumblebee   **bumbar**
boom-bar

butterfly   **leptir**
lep-teer

cab

taksi
tahk-see

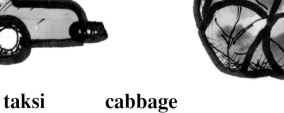

cabbage

zelje
zeliye

cactus

kaktus
kahk-toos

café

kafić
kah-feech

cake

torta
tohr-tah

camel

deva
dehv-ah

camera   **fotoaparat**
fotoh-apah-rat

candle   **svijeća**
sveeye-cha

candy   **bombon**
bohm-bohn

canoe   **kanu**
kah-noo

cap   **kapa**
kah-pah

captain   **kapetan**
kah-peh-tahn

car　　　　　　**auto**
a-ooh-toh

card　　　　　　**karta**
kahr-tah

carpet　　　　　　**tepih**
te-pee-h

carrot　　　　　　**mrkva**
mur-kvah

(to) carry　　　　　　**nositi**
noh-see-tee

castle　　　　　　**dvorac**
dvor-ats

cat　　　　　　　　**mačka**
mah-ch-kah

cave　　　　　　　**pećina**
petch-ee-nah

chair　　　　　　　**stolica**
stoh-lee-tsa

cheese　　　　　　　**sir**
see-rh

cherry　　　　　　　**trešnja**
tresh-nya

chimney　　　　　　**dimnjak**
deem-nyak

chocolate **čokolada**
choh-koh-lada

Christmas tree **Božićna jelka**
boh-zheech-nah yelka

circus **cirkus**
tseer-kuhs

(to) climb **penjati se**
penyaht-ee-se

cloud **oblak**
oh-blahk

clown **klaun**
klown

coach **kočije**
koh-chee-ye

coat **kaput**
kah-puht

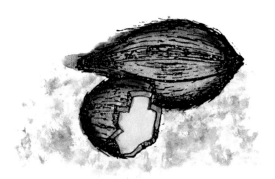

coconut **kokosov orah**
koko-sov o-rah

comb **češalj**
chesh-aly

comforter **poplun**
poh-ploon

compass **kompas**
kom-pass

(to) cook **kuhati**
koo-ha-tee

cork **čep**
chep

corn **kukuruz**
koo-kuhr-ooz

cow **krava**
krah-vah

cracker **kreker**
kreh-ker

cradle **kolijevka**
koh-lee-yevka

(to) crawl   **puzati**
pooh-zah-tee

(to) cross   **prelaziti**
pre-lah-zeeti

crown   **kruna**
kruh-nah

(to) cry   **plakati**
plah-kah-tee

cucumber   **krastavac**
krass-tah-vats

curtain   **zavjesa**
zah-vyesa

(to) dance **plesati**
pleh-sa-tee

dandelion **maslačak**
moss-lah-chak

date **datum**
dah-toom

deer **jelen**
yel-en

desert **pustinja**
poohs-teenya

desk **školska klupa**
sh-kohl-ska kloo-pah

dirty **prljavo**
prly-a-voh

dog

pas
pahs

doghouse

pasja kućica
pahsya kooch-ee-tsa

doll

lutka
loot-ka

dollhouse

kućica za lutke
kooch-ee-tsa zah loot-ke

dolphin

delfin
del-feen

donkey

magarac
mah-gah-rahts

dragon

zmaj
zmay

dragonfly   **konjic**
koh-nyeets

(to) draw   **crtati**
crtaht-ee

dress   **haljina**
ha-lyee-nah

(to) drink   **piti**
pee-tee

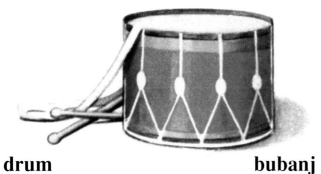

drum   **bubanj**
boo-bany

duck   **patka**
paht-kah

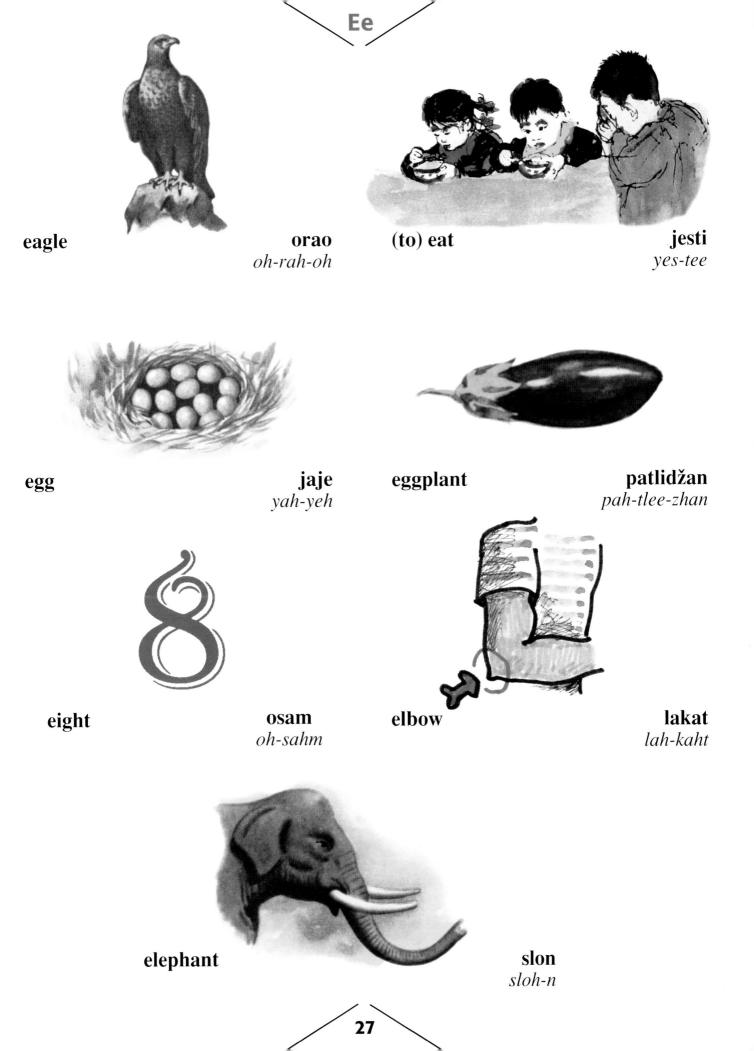

eagle　　　　　　　　**orao**
oh-rah-oh

(to) eat　　　　　　　**jesti**
yes-tee

egg　　　　　　　　　**jaje**
yah-yeh

eggplant　　　　　　　**patlidžan**
pah-tlee-zhan

eight　　　　　　　　**osam**
oh-sahm

elbow　　　　　　　　**lakat**
lah-kaht

elephant　　　　　　　**slon**
sloh-n

empty   **prazno**
prahz-noh

engine   **motor**
moh-tohr

envelope   **kuverta**
kuh-ver-tah

escalator   **pokretne stepenice**
poh-kret-neh steh-pehn-eetse

Eskimo   **Eskim**
eskeem

(to) explore   **istraživati**
ees-tra-zhee-vatee

eye   **oko**
oh-ko

face   **lice**
lee-tse

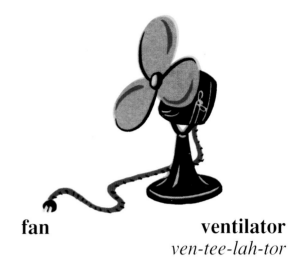

fan   **ventilator**
ven-tee-lah-tor

father   **otac**
o-tats

fear   **strah**
stra-h

feather   **pero**
per-oh

(to) feed   **hraniti**
hra-neet-ee

fence　　　　　　　**ograda**
oh-grah-dah

fern　　　　　　　**paprat**
pap-raht

field　　　　　　　**polje**
polye

field mouse　　　　**poljski miš**
poly-skee-meesh

finger　　　　　　　**prst**
purr-st

fir tree　　　　　　**jela**
yel-lah

fire **vatra**
vat-rah

fish **riba**
ree-bah

(to) fish **pecati**
pets-ah-tee

fist **šaka**
shah-kah

five **pet**
peh-t

flag **zastava**
zah-stav-ah

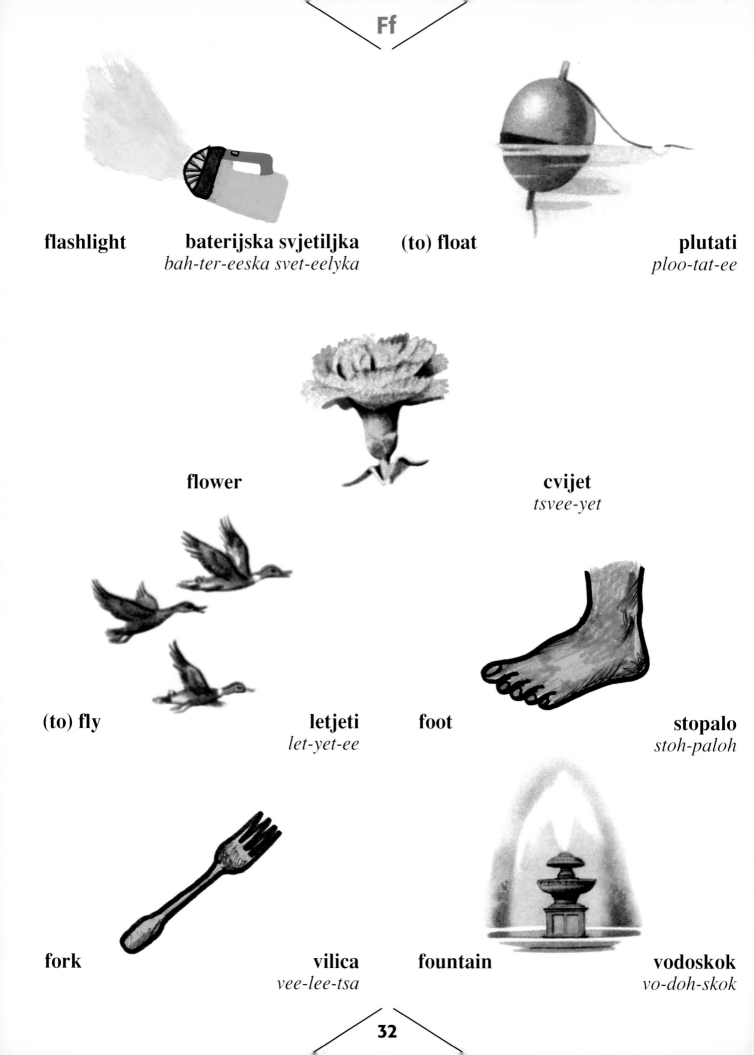

flashlight　**baterijska svjetiljka**
bah-ter-eeska svet-eelyka

(to) float　**plutati**
ploo-tat-ee

flower　**cvijet**
tsvee-yet

(to) fly　**letjeti**
let-yet-ee

foot　**stopalo**
stoh-paloh

fork　**vilica**
vee-lee-tsa

fountain　**vodoskok**
vo-doh-skok

four **četiri**
che-tee-rhee

fox  **lisica**
lee-see-tsa

frame **rama**
rah-mah

friend **prijatelj**
pree-ya-tely

frog **žaba**
zha-bah

fruit **voće**
voh-cheh

furniture **namještaj**
nah-myesh-tahy

garden   **vrt**
vrt

gate   **vrata**
vrah-tah

(to) gather   **skupljati**
skoo-plya-tee

geranium   **geranij**
ger-ahn-eeyee

giraffe   **žirafa**
zhee-rah-fah

girl   **djevojčica**
dye-voy-chee-tsa

(to) give **davati**
dah-vah-tee

glass **čaša**
cha-sha

glasses **naočale**
nah-oh-cha-leh

globe **globus**
glo-boos

glove **rukavica**
ruh-ka-vee-tsa

goat **koza**
koh-zah

goldfish **zlatna ribica**
z-latna ree-bee-tsa

"Good Night" **Laku noć**
lah-koo-noch

"Good-bye" **Doviđenja**
Doh-vee-djenya

goose **guska**
goos-kah

grandfather **djed**
dyed

grandmother **baka**
bah-kah

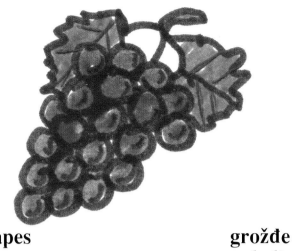

grapes **grožđe**
grozh-dje

grasshopper **skakavac**
skah-kah-vats

green **zeleno**
zel-en-oh

greenhouse **staklenik**
stah-klen-eek

guitar **gitara**
gi-tah-rah

hammer **čekić**
chek-eech

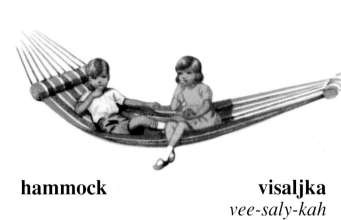

hammock **visaljka**
vee-saly-kah

hamster **hrčak**
her-chak

hand **ruka**
roo-kah

handbag **ženska torbica**
zhen-skah tor-bee-tsa

handkerchief **maramica**
mara-mee-tsa

harvest **berba**
ber-bah

hat **šešir**
shesh-eer

hay **sijeno**
see-yen-oh

headdress **perijanica**
per-ee-yahn-eetsa

heart **srce**
sr-tse

hedgehog **jež**
yezh

hen **kokoš**
koh-kohsh

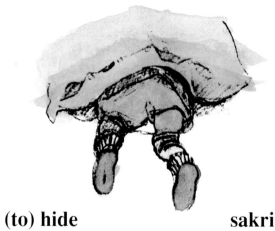

(to) hide **sakriti se**
sah-kree-tee-seh

highway **autocesta**
a-uh-toh tsesta

honey **med**
mehd

horns **rogovi**
roh-goh-vee

horse **konj**
koh-ny

horseshoe   **potkova**
pot-koh-va

hourglass   **pješčani sat**
pyesh-chah-nee saht

house   **kuća**
koo-cha

(to) hug   **zagrliti**
za-grl-ee-tee

hydrant   **hidrant**
he-drant

ice cream   **sladoled**
sla-doh-led

ice cubes   **kocke leda**
kots-keh leh-dah

ice-skating   **klizanje**
klee-zah-nye

instrument   **instrument**
een-stru-ment

iris   **iris**
ee-rees

iron   **glačalo**
gla-cha-loh

island   **otok**
oh-tok

jacket

jakna
yak-nah

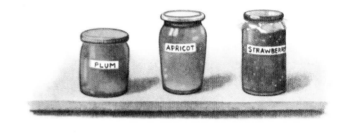

jam

džem
dzh-em

jigsaw puzzle

slagalica
sla-gah-lee-tsa

jockey

džokej
zho-keyh

juggler

žongler
zhon-gler

(to) jump

skakati
ska-kah-tee

kangaroo **klokan**
kloh-kahn

key **ključ**
kly-ooh-ch

kitten **mače**
mat-cheh

knife **nož**
noh-zh

knight **vitez**
vee-tez

(to) knit **plesti**
pless-tee

knot **čvor**
chvor

koala bear **koala**
koh-a-lah

ladder **ljestve**
lyest-veh

ladybug **bubamara**
boo-ba-mara

lamb **janje**
yah-nye

lamp **svjetiljka**
svetily-kah

(to) lap **lokati**
loh-kah-tee

laughter **smijeh**
sm-ee-yeh

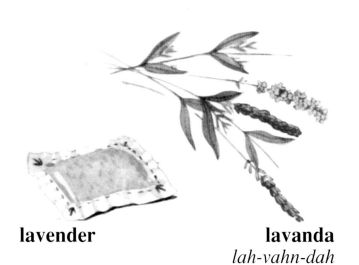

lavender   **lavanda**
lah-vahn-dah

lawn mower   **kosilica**
koh-see-lee-tsa

leaf   **list**
lee-st

leg   **noga**
noh-gah

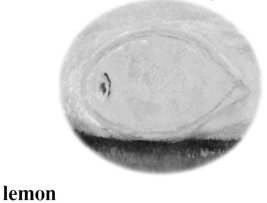

lemon   **limun**
lee-moon

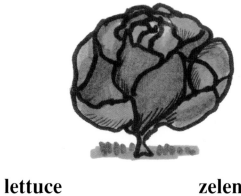

lettuce   **zelena salata**
ze-len-ah sa-lata

lightbulb   **žarulja**
zhar-u-lya

lighthouse   **svjetionik**
svyet-ee-oh-neek

lilac   **jorgovan**
yor-goh-vahn

lion   **lav**
lahv

(to) listen   **slušati**
sloo-sha-tee

lobster   **jastog**
yastog

lock   **brava**
brah-vah

lovebird   **kanarinac**
kah-nah-ree-nats

luggage   **prtljaga**
prtlyaga

lumberjack   **drvosječa**
durvoh-syecha

lunch   **objed**
ob-yed

lynx   **ris**
rees

magazine **časopis**
chas-oh-pees

magician **magičar**
mag-ee-char

magnet **magnet**
mahg-net

map **zemljovid**
zehm-lyo-veed

maple leaf **javorov list**
yavor-ov-leest

marketplace **tržnica**
trzh-nee-tsa

mask **maska**
mah-skah

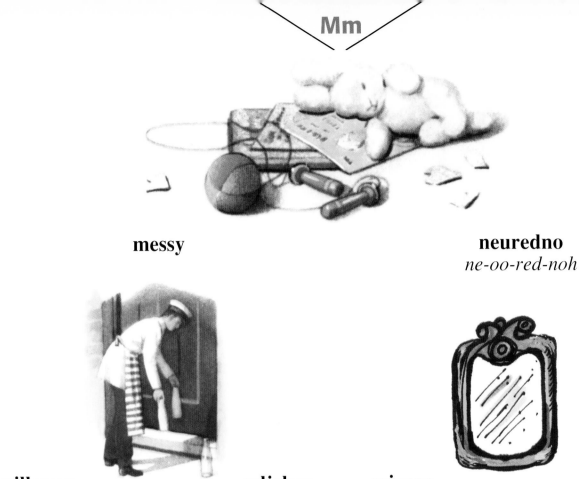

messy **neuredno**
ne-oo-red-noh

milkman **mljekar**
mly-eh-kar

mirror **zrcalo**
zrtsah-loh

mitten **rukavica bez prstiju**
ruh-ka-vee-tsa bez prst-ee-yu

money **novac**
noh-vats

monkey **majmun**
mahy-moon

moon **mjesec**
myes-ets

mother   **majka**
mahy-kah

mountain   **planina**
plah-nee-nah

mouse   **miš**
meesh

mouth   **usta**
ooh-sta

mushroom   **gljiva**
gly-ee-vah

music   **glazba**
glahz-bah

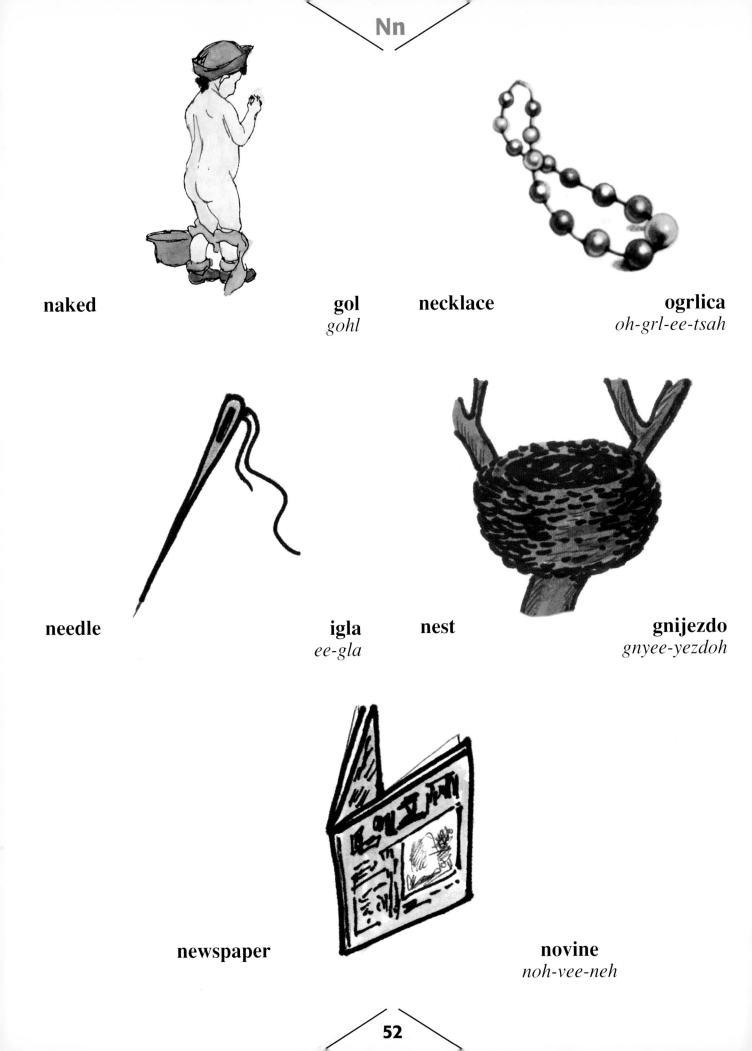

naked   **gol**
                        gohl

necklace   **ogrlica**
                        oh-grl-ee-tsah

needle   **igla**
                        ee-gla

nest   **gnijezdo**
                        gnyee-yezdoh

newspaper   **novine**
                        noh-vee-neh

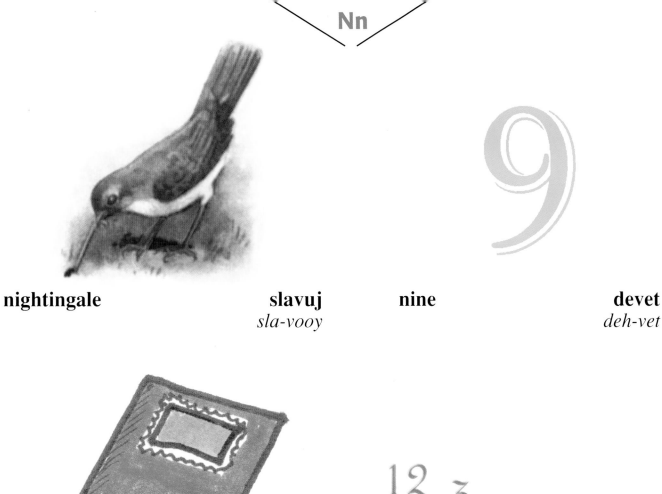

nightingale | **slavuj**
sla-vooy

nine | **devet**
deh-vet

notebook | **bilježnica**
bee-lyezh-nee-tsa

number | **broj**
broh-y

nut | **orah**
oh-rah

oar   **veslo**
                                          vess-loh

ocean liner   **prekooceanski brod**   **old**   **star**
prekoh-oh-tse-yanskee brohd   *stahr*

one   **jedan**   **onion**   **luk**
                   yeh-dan   *loo-k*

open　　　　　**otvoriti**
oh-tvor-ee-tee

orange　　　　　**naranča**
nah-rahn-cha

ostrich　　　　　**noj**
noy

owl　　　　　**sova**
soh-vah

ox　　　　　**vol**
vohl

padlock

lokot
loh-kot

paint

farba
far-bah

painter

slikar
slee-kar

pajamas

pidžama
peed-zhama

palm tree

palma
pahl-mah

paper

papir
pah-peehr

parachute

padobran
pah-doh-bran

park

park
park

parrot

papagaj
pah-pah-guy

passport

putovnica
pooh-tohv-neetsa

patch

zakrpa
zah-kr-pah

path

staza
stah-za

peach

breskva
bress-kva

pear

kruška
kroosh-ka

pebble

šljunak
shlyoo-nak

(to) peck

kljunuti
klyoon-oo-tee

(to) peel

oljuštiti
oly-oo-shtee-tee

pelican

pelikan
pel-ee-kan

pencil

olovka
oh-lov-kah

penguin

pingvin
peehn-gveen

people

narod
nah-rod

piano

klavir
klah-veer

pickle

kiseli krastavac
kee-sel-ee kras-ta-vats

pie

pita
pee-tah

pig

svinja
svee-nya

pigeon

golub
go-loob

pillow

jastuk
yast-ook

pin

pribadača
pree-bah-dah-cha

pine

bor
bore

pineapple

ananas
ah-nah-nas

pit

koštica
kosh-tee-tsa

pitcher

bokal
boh-kahl

plate

tanjur
tany-uhr

platypus

kljunar
klyu-nahr

(to) play   **igrati se**
ee-gra-tee-se

plum   **šljiva**
she-lyee-vah

polar bear   **sjeverni medvjed**
syever-nee med-vyed

pony   **poni**
po-nee

pot   **lonac**
loh-nats

potato   **krumpir**
kroom-peer

(to) pour   **lijevati**
lee-yev-atee

present   **poklon**
poh-klohn

(to) pull   **vući**
voo-chee

pumpkin   **bundeva**
boon-deh-vah

puppy   **štene**
sh-teneh

queen   **kraljica**
kraly-ee-tsa

rabbit

kunić
koon-ee-tch

raccoon

rakun
rah-koon

racket

reket
reh-ket

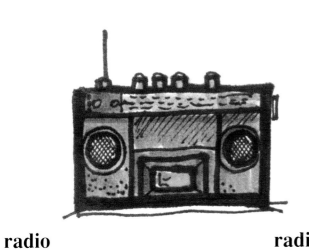

radio

radio
rah-dee-yoh

radish

rotkvica
roht-kvee-tsa

raft   **splav**
sp-lahv

rain   **kiša**
kee-sha

rainbow   **duga**
doo-ga

raincoat   **kični mantil**
kee-shnee man-teel

raspberry   **malina**
mah-leena

(to) read　　　　**pročitati**
proh-chee-ta-tee

red　　　　**crveno**
cr-ve-noh

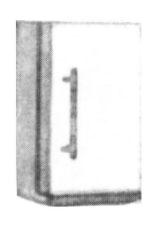

refrigerator　　　　**hladnjak**
hlad-nyak

rhinoceros　　　　**nosorog**
noh-soh-rog

ring　　　　**prsten**
prs-ten

(to) ring　　　　　　**zvoniti**
yvoh-neet-ee

river　　　　　　**rijeka**
ree-ye-ka

road　　　　　　**cesta**
tsest-ah

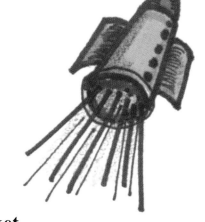

rocket　　　　　　**raketa**
rah-ket-ah

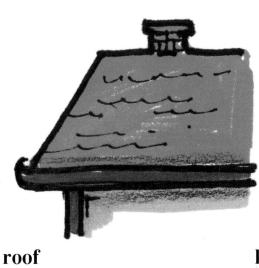

roof　　　　　　**krov**
kr-ov

rooster　　　　　　**pijetao**
pee-ye-ta-oh

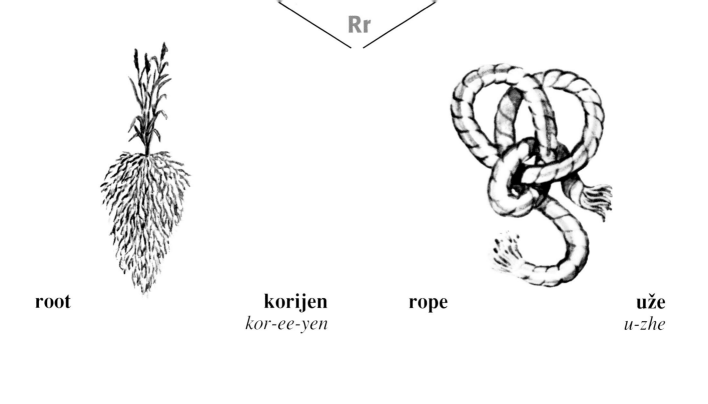

root	**korijen** *kor-ee-yen*
rope	**uže** *u-zhe*

rose	**ruža** *rhu-zha*
(to) row	**veslati** *vess-lah-tee*

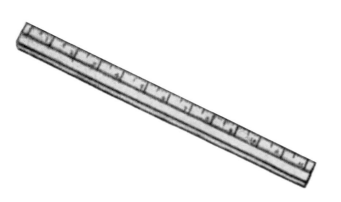

ruler	**ravnalo** *rahv-nah-loh*
(to) run	**trčati** *tur-cha-tee*

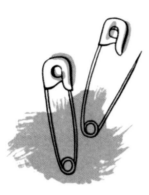

safety pin   **ziherica**
zee-herr-ee-tsa

(to) sail   **jedriti**
yed-ree-tee

sailor   **mornar**
mor-nar

salt   **sol**
sohl

scarf   **šal**
sh-ahl

school   **škola**
sh-koh-lah

scissors   **škare**
sh-kah-reh

screwdriver   **šrafciger**
shraf-tsee-ger

seagull   **galeb**
gah-leb

seesaw   **njihaljka**
nyee-haly-kah

seven   **sedam**
se-dahm

(to) sew   **šiti**
shee-tee

shark   **morski pas**   **sheep**   **ovca**
mor-skee pahs   *ov-tsa*

shell   **školjka**   **shepherd**   **pastir**
shkoly-kah   *pas-teer*

ship   **brod**   **shirt**   **košulja**
brohd   *koh-shoo-lya*

shoe **cipela**
tsee-pel-ah

shovel **lopata**
loh-pat-ah

(to) show **pokazati**
poh-kaz-ah-tee

shower **tuš**
toosh

shutter **prozorski kapak**
proh-zor-skee kah-pak

sick **bolestan**
boh-les-tahn

sieve

sito
see-toh

(to) sing

pjevati
py-e-vah-tee

(to) sit

sjesti
sy-est-ee

six

šest
shest

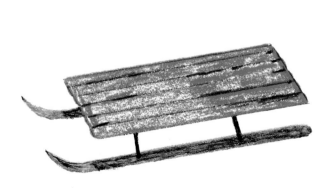

sled

sanjke
sany-keh

(to) sleep

spavati
spah-vah-tee

small　　　　**malen**
mah-lehn

smile　　　　**osmijeh**
oh-smyee-h

snail　　　　**puž**
pooh-zh

snake　　　　**zmija**
z-mee-yah

snow　　　　**snijeg**
snee-yeg

sock　　　　**čarapa**
chah-rah-pah

sofa   **naslonjač**
nah-sloh-nyach

sparrow   **vrabac**
vrah-bah-ts

spider   **pauk**
pah-ook

spiderweb   **paukova mreža**
pah-ook-ova mrezha

spoon   **žlica**
zhl-ee-tsa

squirrel   **vjeverica**
vy-ev-eree-tsatsatsa

stairs　　　　**stube**
stoo-beh

stamp　　　　**poštanska marka**
poh-shtan-ska marka

starfish　　　　**morska zvijezda**
mor-ska zv-ee-jez-dah

stork　　　　**roda**
roh-dah

stove　　　　**šporet**
shpoh-reht

strawberry　　　　**jagoda**
yago-dah

subway　　　　　　　　**podzemna željeznica**
pohd-zem-nah- zhely-ez-nee-tsa

sugar cube　　**šećerna kocka**　　**sun**　　　　　　**sunce**
shech-er-nah kots-kah　　　　　　　　　*soon-tse*

sunflower　　　　　**suncokret**　　**sweater**　　　　**džemper**
soon-tso-kret　　　　　　　　　　　*dzhem-per*

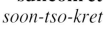

(to) sweep　　　　　　**pomesti**　　**swing**　　　**ljuljačka**
poh-mest-ee　　　　　　　　　　　*lyu-lyach-kah*

table **stol**
stohl

teapot **čajnik**
chay-neek

teddy bear **medvjedić**
med-vyed-eetch

television **televizor**
t*ele-vee-zor*

10

ten **deset**
dess-et

tent **šator**
sha-tor

theater   **kazalište**
kaza-leesh-teh

thimble   **naprstak**
nah-prs-tak

(to) think   **misliti**
mees-lee-tee

three   **tri**
tree

tie   **kravata**
krah-vah-tah

(to) tie   **vezati**
vez-ah-tee

tiger **tigar**
tee-gar

toaster **toster**
toss-ter

tomato **rajčica**
ray-chee-tsa

toucan **tukan**
tooh-kahn

towel **ručnik**
rooch-neekrneek

tower **toranj**
tohr-anye

toy box **kutija za igračke**
koo-tee-ya zah ee-grach-keh

tracks **tračnice**
tratch-nee-tse

train station **kolodvor**
koh-loh-dvor

tray **poslužavnik**
poh-sloozh-av-neek

tree **stablo**
stah-bloh

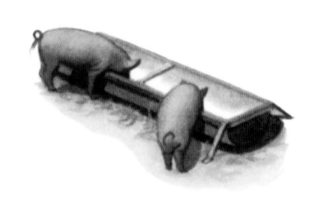

trough **korito**
ko-ree-toh

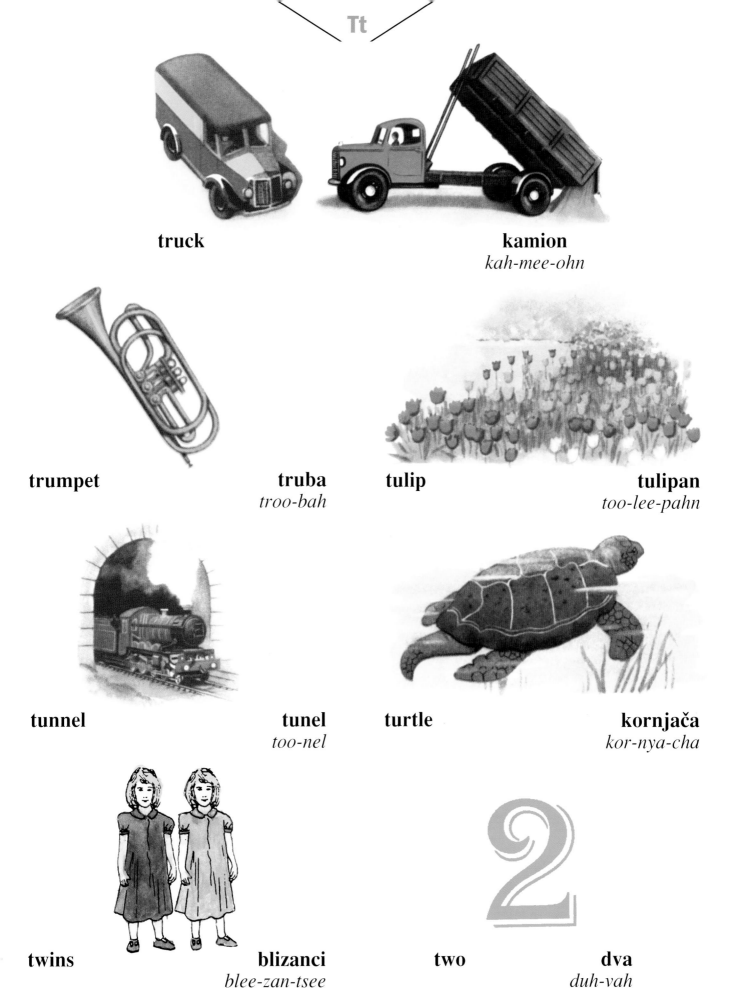

truck

kamion
kah-mee-ohn

trumpet

truba
troo-bah

tulip

tulipan
too-lee-pahn

tunnel

tunel
too-nel

turtle

kornjača
kor-nya-cha

twins

blizanci
blee-zan-tsee

two

dva
duh-vah

umbrella   **kišobran**   **uphill**   **uzbrdo**
keesh-o-brahn   *ooz-br-doh*

vase   **vaza**   **veil**   **veo**
vah-zah   *veh-oh*

village

selo
sel-oh

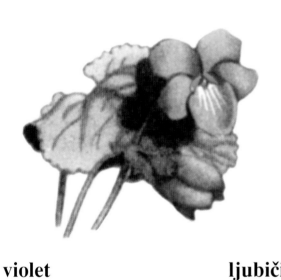

violet

ljubičica
lyu-bee-chee-tsa

violin

violina
veeh-ooh-leeh-nah

voyage

putovanje
pooh-toh-vanye

waiter   **konobar**
koh-noh-bar

(to) wake up   **probuditi se**
proh-bood-ee-tee-seh

walrus   **morž**
mor-zh

(to) wash   **oprati**
oh-prah-tee

watch   **sat**
saht

(to) watch   **gledati**
gle-dah-tee

(to) water   **zaliti**
zah-lee-tee

waterfall   **vodopad**
voh-doh-pahd

watering can   **kanta za zaljevanje**
kan-tah zah zah-lye-vah-nye

watermelon   **lubenica**
loo-ben-ee-tsa

weather vane   **vjetrokaz**
vyetroh-kaz

(to) weigh   **izmjeriti**
eez-myer-ee-tee

whale   **kit**
keet

wheel   **kotač**
koh-tatch

wheelbarrow   **tačke**
tatch-keh

whiskers   **dlake**
dlah-ke

(to) whisper   **šapnuti**
shap-noo-tee

whistle   **zviždaljka**
zveezh-daly-kah

white   **bijelo**
bee-yello

wig   **perika**
per-ee-kah

wind   **vjetar**
vye-tar

window   **prozor**
proh-zor

wings   **krila**
kree-la

winter   **zima**
zee-mah

wolf

vuk
vuh-oo-k

wood   **drvo**   **word**   **riječ**
dr-voh   *ree-yech*

(to) write

pisati
pee-sah-tee

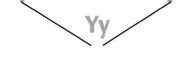

yellow   **žuto**
                             zhoo-toh

Zz

zebra   **zeh-brah**
                             zeh-brah

C

cesta	road
cipela	shoe
cirkus	circus
crno	black
crtati	(to) draw
crveno	red
cvijet	blossom
cvijet	flower

Č

čajnik	teapot
čarapa	sock
časopis	magazine
čaša	glass
čekić	hammer
čep	cork
češalj	comb
četiri	four
četka	brush
čizma	boot
čokolada	chocolate
čvor	knot

A

abeceda	alphabet
akvarij	aquarium
aligator	alligator
ananas	pineapple
antilopa	antelope
auto	car
autocesta	highway

B

bačva	barrel
baka	grandmother
balon	balloon
banana	banana
baterijska svjetiljka	flashlight
beba	baby
berba	harvest
bicikl	bicycle
bijelo	white
bilježnica	notebook
blizanci	twins
boca	bottle
bokal	pitcher
bolestan	sick
bombon	candy
bor	pine
Božićna jelka	Christmas tree
brat	brother
brava	lock
breskva	peach
brod	ship
broj	number
buba	beetle
bubamara	ladybug
bubanj	drum
bumbar	bumblebee
bundeva	pumpkin

D

dabar	beaver
dalekozor	binoculars
datum	date
davati	(to) give
delfin	dolphin
deset	ten
deva	camel
devet	nine
dimnjak	chimney
dječak	boy
djed	grandfather
djevojčica	girl
dlake	whiskers
doručak	breakfast

Dž

džem	jam
džemper	sweater
džokej	jockey

Doviđenja	"Good-bye"
drvo	wood
drvosječa	lumberjack
duga	rainbow
dva	two
dvorac	castle

E

Eskim	Eskimo

F

farba	paint
fotoaparat	camera

G

galeb	seagull
geranij	geranium
gitara	guitar
glačalo	iron
glazba	music
gledati	(to) watch
gljiva	mushroom
globus	globe
gnijezdo	nest
gol	naked
golub	pigeon
grana	branch
grožđe	grapes
guska	goose

H

haljina	dress
hidrant	hydrant
hladnjak	refrigerator
hraniti	(to) feed
hrčak	hamster

I

igla	needle
igrati se	(to) play
instrument	instrument
iris	iris
istraživati	(to) explore
izmjeriti	(to) weigh

J

jabuka	apple
jagoda	strawberry
jaje	egg
jakna	jacket
janje	lamb
jastog	lobster
jastuk	pillow
javorov list	maple leaf
jazavac	badger
ječam	barley
jedan	one
jedriti	(to) sail
jela	fir tree
jelen	deer
jesen	autumn
jesti	(to) eat
jež	hedgehog
jorgovan	lilac

K

kafić	cafe
kaktus	cactus
kamion	truck
kanarinac	lovebird
kanta	bucket
kanta za zaljevanje	watering can
kanu	canoe
kapa	cap
kapetan	captain
kaput	coat
karta	card
kazalište	theater
kiseli krastavac	pickle
kiša	rain
kišni mantil	raincoat
kišobran	umbrella
kit	whale
klaun	clown
klavir	piano
klizanje	ice-skating
ključ	key
kljunar	platypus
kljunuti	(to) peck
klokan	kangaroo
klupa	bench
knjiga	book
koala	koala bear
kocke	blocks
kocke leda	ice cubes
kočije	coach
kokosov orah	coconut
kokoš	hen
kolijevka	cradle
kolodvor	train station
kompas	compass
konj	horse
konjic	dragonfly
konobar	waiter
korijen	root

korito	trough
kornjača	turtle
kosilica	lawn mower
kost	bone
košara	basket
koštica	pit
košulja	shirt
kotač	wheel
koza	goat
kraljica	queen
krastavac	cucumber
krava	cow
kravata	tie
kreker	cracker
krevet	bed
krila	wings
krov	roof
kruh	bread
krumpir	potato
kruna	crown
kruška	pear
kuća	house
kućica za lutke	dollhouse
kuhati	(to) cook
kukuruz	corn
kunić	rabbit
kutija za igračke	toy box
kuverta	envelope

L

lađa	boat
lakat	elbow
Laku noć	"Good night"
lav	lion
lavanda	lavender

mljekar	milkman
mornar	sailor
morska zvijezda	starfish
morski pas	shark
morž	walrus
most	bridge
motor	engine
mrkva	carrot

leptir	butterfly
letjeti	(to) fly
lice	face
lijevati	(to) pour
limun	lemon
lisica	fox
list	leaf
lokati	(to) lap
lokot	padlock
lonac	pot
lopata	shovel
lopta	ball
lubenica	watermelon
luk	arch
luk	onion
lutka	doll

Lj

ljestve	ladder
ljubičica	violet
ljuljačka	swing

M

mače	kitten
mačka	cat
magarac	donkey
magičar	magician
magnet	magnet
majka	mother
majmun	monkey
malen	small
malina	raspberry
maramica	handkerchief
maska	mask
maslačak	dandelion
med	honey
medvjed	bear
medvjedić	teddy bear
metla	broom
misliti	(to) think
miš	mouse
mjesec	moon

N

namještaj	furniture
naočale	glasses
naprstak	thimble
naranča	orange
narod	people
narukvica	bracelet
naslonjač	sofa
neuredno	messy
noga	leg
noj	ostrich
nositi	(to) carry
nosorog	rhinoceros
novac	money
novine	newspaper
nož	knife
njihaljka	seesaw

O

objed	lunch
oblak	cloud
oglasna ploča	bulletin board
ograda	fence
ogrlica	necklace
oko	eye
oljuštiti	(to) peel
olovka	pencil
oprati	(to) wash
orah	nut
orao	eagle
osam	eight

osmijeh	smile
otac	father
otok	island
otvoriti	open
ovca	sheep

P

padobran	parachute
palma	palm tree
papagaj	parrot
papir	paper
paprat	fern
park	park
pas	dog
pasja kućica	doghouse
pastir	shepherd
patka	duck
patlidžan	eggplant
pauk	spider
paukova mreža	spiderweb
pčela	bee
pećina	cave
pecati	(to) fish
pekar	baker
pelikan	pelican
penjati se	(to) climb
perijanica	headdress
perika	wig
pero	feather
pet	five
pidžama	pajamas

Hippocrene Children's Illustrated Foreign Language Dictionaries

Available in 16 languages!

Hippocrene Children's Illustrated Arabic Dictionary
English-Arabic/Arabic-English
94 pages • 8 1/2 x 11 • $11.95pb • 0-7818-0891-X • (212)

Hippocrene Children's Illustrated Chinese Dictionary
English-Chinese/Chinese-English (Mandarin)
94 pages • 8 1/2 x 11 • $11.95pb • 0-7818-0848-0 • (662)

Hippocrene Children's Illustrated Croatian Dictionary
English-Croatian/Croatian-English
94 pages • 8 1/2 x 11 • $11.95pb • 0-7818-1076-0 • (144)

Hippocrene Children's Illustrated Czech Dictionary
English-Czech/Czech-English
94 pages • 8 1/2 x 11 • $11.95pb • 0-7818-0987-8 • (579)

Hippocrene Children's Illustrated Dutch Dictionary
English-Dutch/Dutch-English
94 pages • 8 1/2 x 11 • $11.95pb • 0-7818-0888-X • (175)

Hippocrene Children's Illustrated French Dictionary
English-French/French-English
94 pages • 8 1/2 x 11 • $11.95pb • 0-7818-0847-2 • (663)

Hippocrene Children's Illustrated German Dictionary
English-German/German-English
94 pages • 8 1/2 x 11 • $11.95pb • 0-7818-0986-X • (570)

Hippocrene Children's Illustrated Irish Dictionary
English-Irish/Irish-English
94 pages • 8 1/2 x 11 • $14.95hc • 0-7818-0713-1 • (798)

Hippocrene Children's Illustrated Italian Dictionary
English-Italian/Italian-English
94 pages • 8 1/2 x 11 • $14.95hc • 0-7818-0771-9 • (355)

Hippocrene Children's Illustrated Norwegian Dictionary
English-Norwegian/Norwegian-English
94 pages • 8 1/2 x 11 • $11.95pb • 0-7818-0887-1 • (165)

Hippocrene Children's Illustrated Polish Dictionary
English-Polish/Polish-English
94 pages • 8 1/2 x 11 • $11.95pbi0-7818-0890-1 • (342)

Hippocrene Children's Illustrated Portuguese Dictionary
English-Portuguese/Portuguese-English
94 pages • 8 1/2 x 11 • $11.95pb • 0-7818-0866-3 • (140)

Hippocrene Children's Illustrated Russian Dictionary
English-Russian/Russian-English
94 pages • 8 1/2 x 11 • $11.95pb • 0-7818-0892-8 • (216)

Hippocrene Children's Illustrated Scottish Gaelic Dictionary
English-Scottish Gaelic/Scottish Gaelic-English
94 pages • 8 1/2 x 11 • $14.95hc • 0-7818-0721-2 • (224)

Hippocrene Children's Illustrated Spanish Dictionary
English-Spanish/Spanish-English
94 pages ó 8 1/2 x 11 ó $11.95pb ó 0-7818-0899-8 • (181)

Hippocrene Children's Illustrated Swedish Dictionary
English-Swedish/Swedish-English
94 pages • 8 1/2 x 11 • $11.95pb • 0-7818-0850-2 • (665)

THE HIPPOCRENE LIBRARY OF WORLD FOLKLORE

Folk Tales from Chile
Brenda Hughes
121 pages • 5 1/2 x 8 1/4 • 15 illustrations • 0-7818-0712-3 • $12.50hc • (785)

Folk Tales from Simla
Alice Elizabeth Dracott
225 pages • 5 3/4 x 8 1/2 • 8 illustrations • 0-7818-0704-2 • $14.95hc • (794)

Swedish Fairy Tales
Baron G. Durklou
190 pages • 5 1/2 x 8 1/4 • 21 illustrations • 0-7818-0717-4 • $12.50hc • (787)

Tales of Languedoc: From the South of France
Samuel Jacques Brun
248 pages • 5 1/2 x 8 1/4 • 33 illustrations • 0-7818-0715-8 • $14.95hc • (793)

Prices subject to change without prior notice. To order **Hippocrene Books**, contact your local bookstore, call (718) 454-2366, visit www.hippocrenebooks.com, or write to: Hippocrene Books, 171 Madison Avenue, New York, NY 10016. Please enclose check or money order adding $5.00 shipping (UPS) for the first book and $.50 for each additional title.